A Kingdom's Story

by Jennifer Morillo

Illustrations by Raquel Rodriguez

To order additional copies of this book, contact:
Xlibris
1-888-795-4274
www.Xlibris.com
Orders@Xlibris.com

A Kingdom's Story

by Jennifer Morillo

Illustrations by Raquel Rodriguez

Behind the deepest parts of the woods; dark and foreign, lied a dragon with all its glory. The woods were filled with great treasures, none stolen and most from nature.

The dragon held feasts for all the woodland animals. Even the ones that dug and came in a crawl.

One day these woods were discovered, joy came to a king and a shovel.

The dragon saw these people, and with happiness and joy she soared above the new creatures below.

When she landed with her graceful might, she realized the people were all in a fright.

They found a cave near the edge of the woods. Desolate, rusty, and unused.

For fear of what the dragon might do the people put her in there, scared and bruised.

They chained her there and went on to make their lives. This kingdom's story of how they conquered a dragon became their might.

Other nations would hear in awe how this kingdom had conquered a dragon and still woke with it at dawn.

Years past and the dragon forgot her grace; she did not remember her wings or breath, she even forgot that she wasn't born chained.

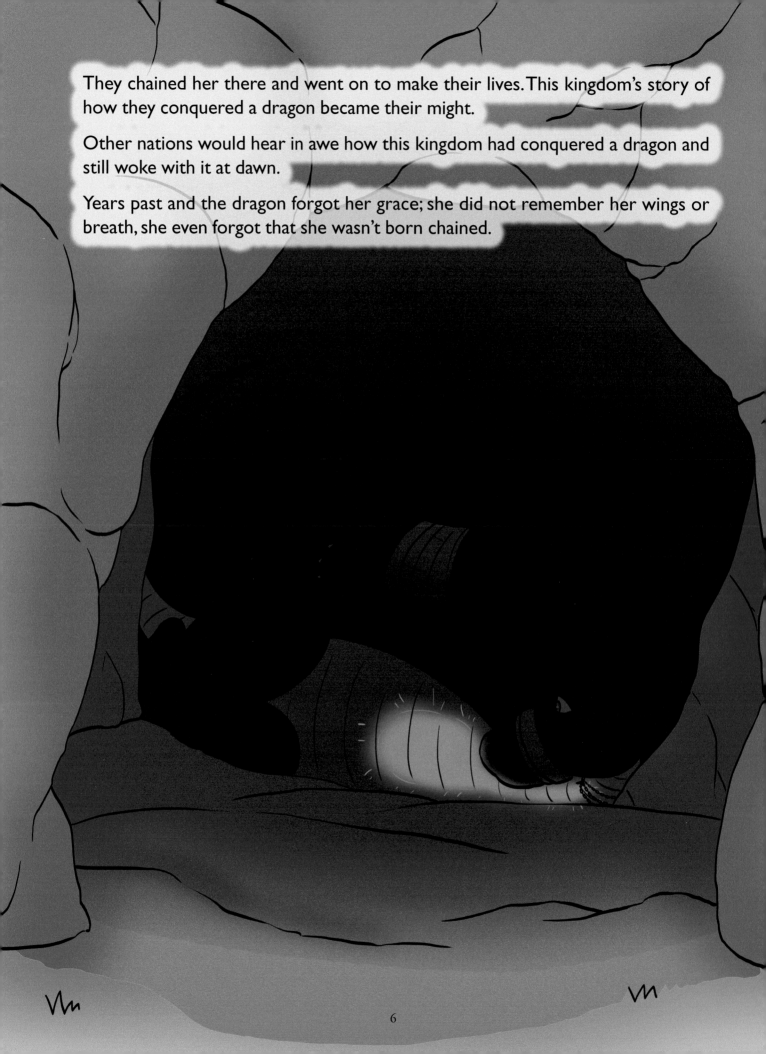

One day someone came into the cave and reminded her, by telling her the story the kingdom told.

She saw her chains and remembered her wings, and for the first time in a long time felt the fire breath that consumed her within.

The kingdom felt a tremble in the night as the dragon pulled the chains off the walls with her might.

They tried to control the dragon and put the chains back, they were being nice. she almost believed they could all be her friend this time.

But she then saw the chains coming back and she became mad at their world.

She peeled her muzzle off and saw again the fear in their eyes, for they knew what would happen when she opened her mouth.

They quickly acted, forgetting the chains and going straight for the dragon's mane.

They all struggled to put the muzzle back on and the dragon shook them all off.

She walked out of the cave that had kept her contained, and with a cry she reminded all who she was in the dead of that night.

They all cried out a warning and a prince dressed in white came to save the fight. He came all high and mighty with a balance in his hands that was oddly off balance.

He threw the balance at the dragon's head, the dragon was speechless and taken aback by this act.

Prince taking this as a sign of the dragon's defeat, thought he won the fight at the dawn of this day.

The dragon, with all her might, broke the clips that tied her wings and with a launch, soared like the wind.

A great wind it created in the kingdom below, knocking the prince right off his horse.

The dragon soared down, and just when the prince was reaching for the balance, she took a deep breath and let the fire out, knocking the balance off the prince's hand.

The balance laid on the ground burned, as the dragon soared above it all.

She flew off to a forest far off where riches grew within the rough. She did feel bad for now the kingdom she left had no balance at all.

So she took some mud and with the fire that she breath, sculpted a new balance with even sides at each end.

And she flew off towards the kingdom again.

She stopped in front of the prince, who trembled with fear, and she laid down the balance she sculpted that year.

The prince looked at the balance with its beauty and size, and asked the dragon for peace as its price.

13

The dragon spread out her wings and the prince went in for a hug smiling.

And so, a new story became this kingdom's might; about a kingdom rebuilt with a dragon by its side.

A kingdom with a new balance and all sleep peacefully at night. And wakes with the grace and might of a dragon, that soars above them, free to be all that she is this time.

The End

Printed in the United States
By Bookmasters